# This Topsy and Tim book belongs to

Anushka nair

Published by Ladybird Books Ltd
80 Strand London WC2R ORL
A Penguin Company

1 3 5 7 9 10 8 6 4 2

# Topsy+Tim

# Busy Builders

**Jean** and **Gareth Adamson**

When Topsy and Tim looked out of the window for the first time on Tuesday morning, they saw a big digger parked at the end of the garden next door.

Mr Fen, who lived next door, came out of his house and said, "Hello," to the man on the digger. Topsy and Tim ran out into their garden and said, "Hello!" too.

"This is my friend, Eric," called Mr Fen
to Topsy and Tim. "Eric and his helpers
are builders. They're going to build
a garage for me, here at the end
of my garden."

"What's the digger for?" asked Tim.
"That's to dig the foundations of
the garage," said Eric.
"Come along, Topsy and Tim,"
called Mummy from the kitchen.
"Time to go to playgroup."

After playgroup, Topsy and Tim hurried home as fast as possible. They couldn't wait to see how the builders were getting on.

The digger had already dug a large,
neat, square hole at the end of
Mr Fen's garden.

When Eric saw Topsy and Tim he called to them, "Hello, twins! Do you think your mum would give us some hot water to make our coffee?"

Topsy and Tim each carried one of the builders' flasks. Each flask had some milk and coffee powder in the bottom.

Mummy poured hot water into the flasks, and they were full of steaming coffee.

Topsy and Tim wanted to help Mummy
take the coffee out to the builders, but
Eric came to the back door to fetch it.
"Come on, twins," he said.
"Come and meet my mates."

Eric's helpers were sitting on a long plank, eating sandwiches and cake. Their names were Joe and Jim. They were pleased to meet Topsy and Tim.

"Have you ever had a ride in
a wheelbarrow?" asked Eric.
He gave Topsy and Tim hard-hats to
wear, and he put a clean sack in the
bottom of the wheelbarrow.

Then he gave them wonderful rides
round and round Mr Fen's garden.
"Time for lunch," called Mummy,
over the garden fence.

While they ate their lunch, Topsy and Tim watched the builders through the kitchen window. They waved to them again and again.

Joe and Jim weren't always looking,
but Eric waved back every time.
After lunch Eric called to them,
"I need two strong workers to help
me shovel some sand!"

Mummy found their seaside spades.
"I'm taking bigger spadefuls!"
said Tim.
"I'm digging faster than you!"
said Topsy.
"You're *both* doing very well!"
said Eric.

At four o'clock Mummy brought
them some apple juice in their own
flasks, and they ate their sandwiches
sitting on the builders' long plank…
because Topsy and Tim were
busy builders, too!

Put the pictures in order
and tell the story.

# Match each one to its home.

Point to the things that begin with the same sound as 'busy' and 'builder'.

Look at the picture.
How many wheelbarrows can
you count?
How many cement mixers?
How many yellow hats?
How many blue hats?